Eight Stories and the
Jewish Values They Teach

It's Too Crowded in Here!

And Other Jewish Folktales

retold for young children by **Vicki L. Weber**   illustrations by **Hector Borlasca**

Behrman House Publishers
www.behrmanhouse.com

D1309699

For Rebecca, Joel, and Ben
with happy memories of bedtime stories
read, re-read, and then read again.

—VLW

Book and Cover design by Stacey May

The stories in *It's Too Crowded in Here!* are based on selected pieces chosen from *Lessons from Our Living Past* (Behrman House) and *Stories from Our Living Past* (Behrman House). Specific original sources are as follows: "It's Too Crowded in Here," Yiddish folktale; "Hillel Takes a Bath," Midrash, Leviticus Rabbah 34:3; "Why Trees Don't Talk," based on "Yossel and the Trees" by Ruth Kozodoy; "The Spider that Saved David," the Second Alphabet of Ben Sira; "The King of Songs," Yalkut Shimoni on Psalm 150; "The Carefree King," Midrash, Leviticus Rabbah 4:6; "The Goat at Made the Stars Sing," Kotzker Rebbe (Menahem Mendel of Kotzk); "The Fishing Lesson," Yiddish folktale.

Parent page material drawn from *Teacher's Guide for Lessons from Our Living Past* by Kelly Cherry with Jules Harlow (Behrman House), and *Teacher's Guide for Stories from Our Living Past* by Arthur C. Blecher with Jules Harlow (Behrman House).

Copyright ©2010 Behrman House, Inc. Springfield, NJ
Manufactured in the United States of America

Library of Congress Cataloguing-in-Publication Data is available.
ISBN 978-874-41850-7

People become the stories they hear and the stories they tell.

—Elie Wiesel

What's Inside

A Note to Parents and Teachers

Why do we read stories to our children? Stories entertain. They charm, excite, even soothe. In the Jewish tradition, stories also teach. Often in the form of an *aggadah*, or parable, they provide an engaging way to pass on our culture and our values, to strengthen our children's Jewish identity. Evolving from the oral tradition that gave us Torah and Talmud, folktales and stories illuminate and reinforce the lessons of our heritage.

The Hebrew poet Bialik wrote that the *aggadah* has become the classic literary form for the artistic expression of the Jewish people in part because they promote spiritual lessons with a certain practical wisdom that always retains 'the scent of the earth.'

> "The beautiful palace which the *aggadah* has built with the creative strength of many generations—we do not view it as a museum of antiquities, where a person enters, looks around, and leaves. Rather it serves as a permanent home for the spirit and soul of our people."
>
> Bialik, Preface to *The Sefer Ha-aggadah*

It's Too Crowded in Here! is a collection of Jewish folktales and midrashic stories in this spirit, retold for young children and enlivened by detailed, colorful illustrations. Fun just to read aloud with your children, the stories also provide a rich yet light-hearted resource for exploring key values such as self respect, compassion, appreciation, tolerance, and thankfulness.

To help you, at the end of each story you will find a resource page for parents and teachers. This page provides some brief background linking the story with its underlying message and connecting it to sources in Jewish tradition. Whatever your own background or level of Jewish knowledge, these supplemental notes, together with a few open-ended questions and activity suggestions based on each story, can help you if you would like to lead your children through a deeper exploration of each story.

It's Too Crowded in Here!

Once, long ago a farmer and his wife lived in a teeny, tiny house with their great, big family. Their teeny, tiny house was very, very crowded.

How crowded was it? It was so crowded that the only way to fit the whole family around the table for Shabbat dinner was to put the smaller children on the laps of the bigger children, and put the baby in the sink. It was so crowded that at night, the children who could not fit into the one tiny bed took turns sleeping in the dresser drawers.

At last, the farmer and his wife could stand it no longer. They walked into the village and asked to see the rabbi. "What can we do about our teeny, tiny house?" they asked. "It's too crowded in there!"

The rabbi sat back in his chair, closed his eyes, and stroked his long beard. He looked very wise as he sat and thought. "Ahh," the rabbi said at last, sitting up in his chair with a sparkle in his eye. "I will tell you what to do. Go home now and bring one of your chickens into the house to live with you and your family."

The farmer and his wife did not know how a chicken would help, but they trusted the rabbi, so they went home and did as he said.

As soon as they let the chicken loose inside, it squawked and flapped and fluttered around the tiny room. The children jumped, and everyone tried to stay

away from the squawking, flapping chicken but there was no place to go. "It's too crowded in here!" the farmer cried as the chicken landed on his head.

So the farmer and his wife went back to see the rabbi. "The chicken is only making things worse," they told him.

"Ahh," said the rabbi. "In that case, you need to bring your goat inside to live with you and your family and your chicken."

When the farmer and his wife brought the goat inside, it bleated and butted and banged around the tiny room. It crunched the farmer's cap and tried to eat the chicken's feathers. It munched the children's jackets and their mother's apron. The children jumped and the chicken flapped, and everyone tried to stay away from the munching, crunching goat. "It's too crowded in here!" shouted the children.

So the farmer and his wife went back to the rabbi again.

"Ahh," said the rabbi. "You need to bring your cow inside to live with you and your family and your chicken and your goat."

To get the cow into the teeny, tiny house, the farmer had to push from behind while the farmer's wife pulled from the front. The children pressed up against the wall to make room.

The chicken squawked and flapped and fluttered onto the cow's back. The cow mooed and chewed and shook its head. The goat butted and banged and ran under the table, munching someone's shoe.

The table wiggled and wobbled and the Shabbat candlesticks tumbled. The farmer caught them just before they crashed to the floor. "It's too crowded in here!" shouted the farmer's wife.

The farmer and his wife crawled under the cow to get out of the house, and went back to see the rabbi.

"Rabbi," they said. "There is no room to live. There is no room to move. There is no room to *breathe*."

"Ahh," said the rabbi. "Do not worry. Go back home my friends. Go lead your cow back out to the pasture. Go let your goat back into the yard. Go put your chicken back in its coop. Then see what happens."

The farmer and his wife trudged back home. They led the cow back to the pasture. They let the goat back into the yard. They put the chicken back in the coop. Then they went into their teeny, tiny house, and discovered something amazing.

Their house felt as large as a palace!

And so the farmer and his wife and all their family lived the rest of their days, happy and content in their great big, teeny tiny house.

Is the glass half empty or half full? There is an old world sensibility to the wisdom of this classic folktale in which 'bad' seems good when compared to worse. It does remind us, though, that perspective is important in life if we wish to achieve a measure of contentment. In a world in which it sometimes seems that we should always be looking for more, there can be genuine satisfaction in saying "this is enough."

What makes contentment a Jewish value? In this story, true wealth comes from self-acceptance. "Who is rich?" we are asked, "Those who are content with their lot in life" (*Mishnah, Avot 4.1*). How often have we seen others engulfed in discontent because of an acute awareness of the things they don't have? Our children may get frustrated by our refusal to indulge them by buying anything they may want. Yet rewarding them with time and attention instead may offer them a clearer sense of self-worth and true wealth.

Attitude adjustments. "It's Too Crowded in Here" is framed in a comic and clever way that helps us see that it is possible for us to change our perception of reality. The family's environment has not changed, but their attitude has altered dramatically. A second important lesson is that we sometimes learn best through life encounters—by doing. The village rabbi refrains from dispensing advice to the farmer and his wife. He has them act out the lesson he wants them to learn. He models for them a way to teach themselves through action and observation, rather than simply by listening passively to advice.

Quizzical Questions

1. What do you do or have right now that makes you happy?

2. What would happen if you got every single thing you asked for?

Try This!

Think of ten people you know. Imagine they are coming to live with you in your house! Describe where each one will sit or sleep so that everyone will fit. What would be harder about having so many people live in your house? What would be easier? What would be more fun?

Now you try: Have as many people in your family as you can crowd together in one chair, or on one bed, to read a story. First describe what is uncomfortable. Then describe what is nice.

Hillel
Takes a
Bath

Rabbi Hillel came to school one day with a large linen cloth on his shoulder and a twinkle in his eye.

"Today I will use this cloth to do a mitzvah," he said to his class. He whisked the cloth off his shoulder and snapped it in the air. "What do you think I will do?"

The rabbi's students were puzzled and delighted. They never knew from one day to the next what their teacher would do in order to help them learn to follow God's ways. Why, one time a man challenged Rabbi Hillel to teach him the whole of the Torah while standing on one foot—and their wise and mischievous teacher was able to do it in just one sentence!

They students whispered together to find an answer.

"Will you give it to a poor man to use as a blanket?" asked one.

"Giving tzedakah is an important mitzvah," said Rabbi Hillel. "It reminds us that everyone deserves justice and mercy in God's world. But that is not what I will do with this cloth today."

"Will you spread it on your table to get it ready for Shabbat?" asked another.

"Keeping Shabbat is an important mitzvah," said Rabbi Hillel. "It reminds us that we must keep our holy day special to honor God. But that is not what I will do with this cloth today."

"Will you make it into a tent, so that your parents can sit in the cool shade?" asked a third.

"Honoring one's parents is an important mitzvah," said Rabbi Hillel. "It reminds us of everything that God commanded at Mount Sinai. But that is not what I will do with this cloth today."

The students thought and talked. They talked and thought. For each new answer, Rabbi Hillel praised them for thinking of an important mitzvah. "But that is not what I will do with this cloth today," he said.

At last, the students could think of nothing more.

"Tell us, Rabbi," they pleaded. "What other mitzvah can you possibly do with your cloth?"

"Ah," said Rabbi Hillel. "Today I will use this cloth to dry myself after I take a bath."

"Take a bath!" exclaimed the surprised students. "How can taking a bath be a mitzvah?"

"Ah," said Rabbi Hillel. "Let's think about that while we take a walk."

Rabbi Hillel picked up his cloth and led his students out of the classroom. They walked through the city until they came to the marketplace. It was an open, busy plaza where people of the city came every day to buy and sell and conduct their business.

"Look," Rabbi Hillel said to his students. "Tell me what you see at the end of the plaza."

"It is a statue of the king," said one of the students.

"And what are the workers doing?" asked Rabbi Hillel.

"They are cleaning the statue," said another student.

"And why do you think the workers are cleaning the statue of the king?" Rabbi Hillel asked.

"Well," said one student, "The statue is made in the image of the king. If the people allowed it to become dirty, it would show lack of respect for the king."

"So," said Rabbi Hillel. "These people work hard every day to keep this statue gleaming in order to honor the king."

Rabbi Hillel paused for a moment before asking his next question. He wanted his students' full attention.

"And in whose image are we made, you and I?" he asked.

All the students answered together, for they had learned this lesson well. "We are made in God's image."

"Yes!" said Rabbi Hillel. "So how can I use this cloth to honor God?"

"You can take a bath!" laughed the students.

"Right!" said Rabbi Hillel. "When we keep ourselves clean, we honor God. And that is why taking a bath is an important mitzvah."

Rabbi Hillel smiled at his students and sent them home. And then he went to take his bath.

We Treat Ourselves with Respect

What's a mitzvah? The surprise in this story is that such an everyday part of life as bathing is also a mitzvah. A mitzvah is a commandment, one of 613 specific acts described in the Torah. And although mitzvot are not simply "good deeds," the word mitzvah has also come to mean an act of human kindness.

What makes self-respect a Jewish value? We are instructed to "love your neighbor as yourself." Yet we can only embrace others when we first know what it is to love ourselves. For children, self-respect can first be understood in terms of self-care.

How do I explain "made in God's image?" The Talmud says "wash your face, hands, and feet daily in honor of your Maker." The concept of people made in God's image can be a challenge for young children. We can explain that we do not mean we look like God, for we do not know what God might look like. We can encourage them to guess at the meaning. Do we have gifts or talents, wisdom or goodness that resembles, even faintly, the wisdom and goodness we ascribe to God? Do we have the ability—like God—to know right from wrong? And if we have qualities that we believe reflect God, where are they housed? Why are our bodies important?

Don't Forget the Fun! Of course, we could simply avoid messiness. But denying ourselves fun—even the fun of getting dirty—is not the point. The Talmud also tells us that "you will have to give a reckoning for the joys of life that you failed to experience."

Quizzical Questions

1. What is your favorite way to get dirty?

2. Why not just stay dirty?

3. How do you show you like a friend?

4. How do you show you like yourself?

Try This!

The great Rabbi Hillel was once challenged to teach the entire Torah while standing on one foot. Rabbi Hillel said, "What you do not like done to you, do not do to others. The rest is explanation; go and study."

How does liking yourself help you do as Rabbi Hillel taught? What is the first thing you need to know in order to follow this "golden rule"?

Now you try: Stand on one foot and recite Rabbi Hillel's golden rule.

Why Trees Don't Talk

Once there was a little village surrounded by a lovely orchard. The fruit from this orchard was so sweet, so juicy, and so delicious that it was famous throughout the land.

The villagers were proud of their orchard. They took care of the trees. They pruned the branches, raked the leaves, and protected the fruit from the passing birds. In the fall they picked the ripe fruit from the branches, and

gathered the fallen pieces from the ground. It was hard work, but everyone helped.

Everyone that is, except for Golde.

Golde always meant to help. "Today I am going to the orchard to help pick fruit," she said to her neighbor as she fed her chickens. "My father taught me the secret to picking, and I am sure I can pick faster than anyone."

Golde started down the road toward the orchard. As she passed the bakery she stopped to talk to the women who were waiting for their dough to bake. "I am going to pick fruit today," she told them.

"I am sure I can pick faster than anyone. My father told me the secret to picking." Golde and the other women argued a bit about the best way to pick and then Golde told them about the best way to make bread. (Golde's mother had told her a special secret for that.)

Golde talked and talked, and before she knew it all the bread came out of the oven and the other women disappeared back to their houses. So Golde walked on. She passed the tailor's shop. The tailor was sewing a new button on a man's coat.

"I am on my way to help pick fruit," Golde told the tailor and his customer. "I am sure I can pick faster than anyone. My father told me the secret to picking." Golde and the tailor and his customer argued about the best way to pick fruit, and then Golde told the tailor about the best way to sew a button onto a coat. (Golde's grandmother had told her a special secret for sewing on buttons.)

Golde walked on and on through the village. Each time

she met one of her neighbors, Golde boasted about how fast she could pick fruit. And whether the neighbor was milking a cow or grinding grain or herding goats down the road, Golde always stopped to tell them how to do it better.

When Golde finally reached the orchard, it was very late. She was tired and hungry. Golde had been talking

so much that her throat was dry and scratchy. She looked at the beautiful ripe fruit hanging just above her head, and picked an apron full. Then she sat down and ate every single piece. It was delicious! Golde sat happily under the tree, looking up through the leaves.

"You know the secret for making wonderful fruit," Golde said to the tree. "Why don't you talk? Then you could tell everyone how you do it!"

And to her surprise, the tree replied. "I don't have to talk about myself, or even talk at all," it said. "I offer sweet, delicious fruit. My fruit speaks for me, and that is enough."

We Help by Getting Things Done

Actions speak louder than words. Intentions—even the best ones—are of little use when they are not followed by action. Golde's chattering and baseless boasting stand in sharp contrast to the silent productivity of the trees, whose fruit is the source of the town's deep civic pride. The contrast demonstrates how behavior reveals character. Action brings results and respect. Talk alone creates nothing.

What makes action a Jewish value? The emphasis on action is an important part of Jewish heritage. A midrash on Exodus 24:7 teaches that God offered the Torah to many nations before coming to the Israelites. Each nation first wanted to hear what they would have to do once they accepted the Torah, and each nation found its codes and requirements too stringent. Then God came to the Israelites and offered the Torah. They replied, "All that God has spoken, we will do and we will hear."

The Bible's attitude toward trees. The Bible pays particular attention to trees. The Middle East is not heavily wooded and in ancient times trees were highly prized for their shade, their fruit, and for indicating the location of sources of water. One of the admonitions in the Bible is: "Only trees which are not for food may you cut down for protection against the city that makes war with you" (*Deuteronomy 20:20*). In addition to serving as a symbol of environmentalism, trees also serve as a metaphor for our care of future generations because of their long life span and because many fruit trees take years after planting to become productive. "Just as when you entered the land you found others have planted before you, so shall you plant for the sake of your children (*Talmud, Taanit 23a*)."

Quizzical Questions

1. What do you do well?
2. How do you know?
3. How did you get better?
4. What do you wish you could do?

Try This!

It's easier to get something done when you have a plan. You can divide a big job into smaller steps.

Now you try: Think of a big job you need to do. Perhaps you need to clean your room. What are three steps you can take to get it done?

The Spider that Saved David

Long before he became king of Israel, David was famous. We know he killed Goliath the giant when everyone else was afraid to fight. He had many other adventures as well. And sometimes his fame got David into trouble.

One day as he walked in the woods, David saw a spider spinning its web between the

branches
of a tree.
He stopped and sat
beneath the tree to
watch the spider's quick
and careful work. The web
was so intricate, the spider so
diligent.

But just as the web was nearly
finished, a gust of wind blew through
the trees. It bent the tree's branches,
tore off some of the leaves, and left the
spider's web
in tatters.

David rolled his eyes and shook his head.
"What a waste," he sneered. "Why bother with a
creature that spends all its time making something
so flimsy and useless?"

As he stood up to leave, David heard someone calling to him through the wood. It was his friend Jonathan, the son of King Saul.

"David!" cried Jonathan. "You must run! My father is sending his soldiers to find you. He is angry because his people love you so much. He thinks you will try to steal his throne. Run now and hide!"

And so David ran. He ran through the woods. He ran down from the mountains. He ran into the desert. The armies of King Saul followed, searching for him at every step. There was no place for David to hide, so on and on he ran.

When he reached the rocky wilderness of Ein Gedi, David was exhausted and

afraid. There was no place left to go. Just as he was about to give up, David spied an opening in the rock. He wriggled through into a small cave. There, huddled in the dark and worn out from the running, David fell asleep.

The thunder of horses' hooves startled David awake. King Saul's army! The hoof beats stopped. David sat very still. He heard the crunch of footsteps near the mouth of his little cave. He held his breath.

His heart pounded so hard in his chest he was sure the soldiers would hear it.

"Never mind," shouted one of the soldiers. "He can't be in there. There is a huge spider web in front of this cave. No one could have gotten past without ripping it," he said.

David looked up in surprise and saw that it was true. While he was asleep a spider had come and spun a web that completely covered the entrance to his hiding place. The spider and its delicate web had saved him! And so David, safe and snug, sat awhile and watched the spider work.

We Find Ways to Appreciate Others

Future king meets spider. This midrashic tale of adventure and pursuit is characteristic of numerous rabbinic traditions about David. The stories exaggerate further the exemplary qualities attributed to David in biblical accounts as handsome, popular, talented, and astute. And yet, in the rabbinic literature David's life is saved over and over by a variety of animals—a deer, a lion, even a wasp, and in this story, a spider. The message: even the lowliest have something to contribute. They can even save a king.

What makes appreciation a Jewish value? From its very beginning, the Bible contains expressions of appreciation. In Genesis, at the creation of the world, "God saw that it was good." And our sages wryly interpreted the order of the world's biblical beginnings as a way to underscore our need to develop a sense of appreciation: "So that should a person become too proud, one could say, 'A gnat preceded you in Creation' " (*Talmud, Sanhedrin 38a*).

How can I help my child develop appreciation for others? Nature is a doorway to appreciation, especially for young children. It is hard to look at a spider's web and not marvel that so tiny a creature can produce such an intricate structure. In drawing our children's attention to the natural world, we help them develop appreciation and respect for the diversity of life. By highlighting the roles various creatures play in our world, we can help children understand that even those creatures that we are not immediately drawn to have a contribution to make.

Quizzical Questions

1. What is your favorite animal?

2. What is an animal you don't like?

3. Why do we like some animals and not others?

4. How can we show that we appreciate a spider? An ant?

5. How can we show that we appreciate a person?

Try This!

Some animals, like puppies and bunnies, are easy to like and appreciate. Others are unusual or odd looking. Some are even scary. What are some animals that might be hard to like?

Now you try: Pretend you are one of these hard-to-like animals. What do you look like? What do you do? What is your special role in the world?

The King
of Songs

King David had a harp that he kept on the wall above his bed. Often at midnight the wind came in the window and whispered through the harp strings, playing a quiet song.

David always woke when he heard the wind in his harp. Then he would take the harp down from its hook on the wall and play it himself while the wind quietly whistled along. The songs David played were all songs he had written himself. Deep into the night David played and sang his songs to God.

Sometimes David sang songs of joy that told of the wonders of the world and how good it is to be alive. Sometimes the songs were full of thanks to God, and praise for God's justice and mercy. In times of trouble, David's songs asked God for help and understanding. But the songs were always beautiful, because they told David's deepest, truest feelings.

One night as David strummed lightly on his harp, he found himself making up a brand new song. He played and sang the tune again and again. It was perfect! David was so excited about his new song, and so proud of

it that he put down his harp, jumped up to his window and shouted into the night, "There is no one else in God's wide world who can sing songs as wonderful as mine!"

David's words echoed through the moonlit night. As they died away the only sound left was the croaking of the frogs in their pond near the gate of the palace. As David stood at the window the croaking grew louder and louder. Suddenly, with a whoosh and plop and a big fat splat, a large green bullfrog hurtled past David and landed wetly on the floor in the middle of the room.

"CROAK!" said the frog, filling the whole room with its deep, rumbling voice.

The startled David turned around to face the frog. He put his hands on his hips and stared in amazement at this bold creature who had invaded his bedroom. But the frog, sitting on the floor with its giant eyes half closed, seemed cool and calm, not even afraid of a king. Its tongue whipped out and grabbed a passing fly. It swallowed with a loud gulp and then, to David's astonishment, it spoke.

"King David," said the frog. "Do not think you are the only fine singer of songs. My family and I have been

singing our own wonderful songs to God long before you were born!" The frog let out one last "CROAK," jumped to the windowsill and out into the night, disappearing almost as quickly as he had come.

Hands still on his hips, David stood perfectly still, staring through the empty window after the frog. He was much too surprised to know what to think.

Finally, he picked up his harp and carefully hung it on its hook on the wall. As he got back into bed, David smiled. Then he lay down, closed his eyes, and listened to the songs of the bullfrogs in the night.

We Accept Differences in Each Other

Stop, look, and listen. Happily, the bullfrog in this story has no self-esteem issues. He has no qualms about correcting a king, or insisting that David acknowledge the value and beauty of his talents and those of his kin. His surprising intrusion into David's room as well as his song forces David to stop, to listen, and to begin to understand. We live in a multi-cultural society. We can miss the beauty in other songs, other voices, other ways of living that are different from our own unless we take a moment to pay attention, to share our similarities and understand our differences.

What makes tolerance a Jewish value? Listening between people is valued in Judaism for its role in developing compassion and understanding, which leads to becoming open-minded and unbiased in our dealings with others. And yet it is challenging to listen equally to all people without bias. "If a poor person comes, and pleads before another, that other does not listen. If someone who is rich comes, that person is received at once. God does not act in such a manner. All are equal before God" (*Exodus Rabbah 21:4*).

Difference discoveries. Through directed observation we can help young children discover that differences among people are a source of richness in our world. Have them think carefully about someone they know. Ask them: how are the two of you different? (Hair, eyes, dress, likes and dislikes, skills?) How are the two of you alike? Describe something about the other person that you admire, or something that person can do that you would like to learn more about. What question would you want to ask?

Quizzical Questions

1. Who is the best listener you know?

2. How can you tell?

3. How do you show you are listening?

4. How can you use your eyes to listen?

Try This!

When is it impossible to listen? When you are talking yourself!

Now you try: How long can you go without talking? Be silent for as long as you can. Listen carefully. Pay attention to all the things you can hear. What are they?

The Carefree King

Once long ago, in a land far away, a king lived in happy splendor in a beautiful palace surrounded by high walls and a wide, deep moat.

Inside the walls, the land around the palace was fertile and lush. There were golden fields of plump grain, bountiful gardens bursting with ripe red tomatoes and sweet yellow corn, and fruit trees heavy with crisp apples and juicy pears. The king loved to walk through his beautiful garden, his orchards, and his fields. He and his royal court ate well because of the bounty of the palace lands.

Outside the walls of the palace, the land was dry and hard, and full of stones. The people of the kingdom worked hard, but very little grew in the dusty earth. The grain shriveled on its stalks. The tomato plants withered and the ears of corn were tiny and parched. The flowers on the fruit trees dried up and blew away, never setting any fruit.

"The gardens and the orchards outside the palace are dying, your majesty," said one of the king's advisors.

"Why worry?" asked the king. "My own gardens here in the palace grow more beautiful every day, and I have apples and pears aplenty. I will be fine."

"The fields of grain outside the palace will not grow," said the advisor.

"Why worry?" asked the king. "My own fields inside the palace walls grow more grain than ever. I will have plenty of bread. I will be fine." And the king went out to walk in his beautiful garden.

As the king walked, he passed some of the villagers who worked daily in his garden pulling weeds, shooing away the birds, and picking vegetables for the king's table. They looked down as the king passed. They were unhappy working in the king's garden when nothing would grow in their own.

But one old woman did not look down. She lifted her head and called out to the king.

"Your majesty," she called out, her voice tired and trembling. "You have a beautiful garden. It would be even more beautiful with a little pond in the middle."

"What a lovely idea," said the king. "A pond in the middle of my garden!"

"Yes," said the old woman, her voice growing stronger. "And it would be even nicer if it had a few fish. I have seen beautiful fish in your moat when I come to the palace to work in your garden."

"Fish!" said the king. "Wonderful! But I have never seen fish in my moat."

"I can show you where they are," said the old woman. "My husband once worked at the palace. He fixed the cracks in the walls of the moat. He kept a little boat. I know how to row it."

And so the old woman picked up her shawl from the ground and led the king to the edge of the moat, where they found the little boat. The king sat up in the front. The old woman sat behind, put her shawl on the seat beside her, and began to row. When they reached the middle of the moat, she stopped. She was breathing very hard, and looked very tired.

The king peered over the front of the boat. "I cannot see any fish," he said. "Are you sure they are here?"

"Keep looking," said the old woman. As the king leaned over to look deeper into the water, the old woman pulled a large awl out from under her shawl. With its sharp tip she began to chip a hole in the bottom of the little boat.

The king looked back in surprise. "Old woman!" he cried. "What on earth are you doing?"

"I am old," said the woman. "My husband has died. I have no children. I work all day in the palace garden. I go home tired and hungry every night. My house is empty and my own garden is dying. I am too old, too tired and too hungry to go on. I don't feel like living anymore."

"But you are putting a hole in the boat! What about me? I don't want to die!" exclaimed the king, now terrified.

"Why worry, your majesty?" asked the old woman. "You will not have a hole in your end of the boat. You will be fine."

The king suddenly laughed, his terror forgotten. "I see what you are really trying to show me," he said, with kindness in his voice for the very first time. "Now, let me row us back to shore. Today I will open the palace gardens to all my people, and everyone will have plenty to eat. And then we will use the water in this moat to make all the gardens in the land lush and green and bountiful for all of us."

And they did.

We Depend on One Another

We're all in the same boat. In a rather literal illustration of this classic aphorism, an elderly woman in difficult circumstances demonstrates the power of 'experiential learning.' Jewish heritage has many stories of the haughty learning from the humble. "Who is wise?" we are asked. "One who learns from every person" (*Mishnah, Avot 4:1*).

What makes cooperation a Jewish value? The king in this story thought his personal circumstances made him exempt from worrying about the misery around him. Yet the lessons of Judaism often connect the responsibilities we have to ourselves with the responsibilities we have to other people. We are meant to understand that each of us is a part of a greater whole, and that each person's destiny depends upon the fate of others as well. Both the individual and the community are worthy of our care. "If I am not for myself who will be for me? If I am only for myself what am I?" (*Mishnah, Avot 1:14*). The tension between self and other keeps our ethical world in balance, and flows from Judaism's basic ethic, "Love your neighbor as yourself" (*Leviticus 19:18*).

Fairness through teamwork. Young children have a basic sense of fairness that will likely be violated by the behavior of the king in this story. His selfishness led to others' distress. Yet 'sharing' is only a part of the solution. In becoming willing to work together with his subjects, the king opened the way to a stronger as well as a more equitable kingdom.

Quizzical Questions

1. What is your favorite game to play alone?

2. What games are impossible to play alone?

Try This!

Have you ever played tug of war? Two teams hold the opposite ends of a long rope. At the signal each team tries to pull the other team over a line in the middle. Is there a way everybody can win playing tug of war?

Now you try: Both teams hold on to the rope and sit on the ground facing each other. Everyone PULLS as hard as they can. As you pull, everyone begins to stand up. When everyone on both teams is standing up, you all win! It's a tug of peace! You can even try this with two people holding hands—pull yourselves up together!

The Goat that Made the Stars Sing

Once there was an unusual goat with silky black ears, flowing white hair, and long golden horns. The goat's horns were so long they reached all the way to the sky. Each evening after the sun went down the goat walked to a high hill and looked up at the stars in the night sky. One by one, he gently tapped them with his golden horns. As he tapped, each

star began to sing, until all the stars in the heavens had joined into one beautiful bedtime chorus. In this way all the people of the world fell asleep each night listening to the lullaby of the stars.

One day, as the goat was grazing in a field near his hill, he saw a young man angrily kicking stones across the road. "What is the matter?" asked the goat.

"I am so upset!" said the young man, not even looking up. "I had a little box, a little box for salt. I lost it and now I cannot carry my salt with me as I travel from place to place."

The young man looked up from his search along the road, and saw the goat. "Oh my!" he said. "You are the goat that makes the stars sing! Your horns are so very long. I am sure they are more than long enough

to touch the stars. May I please have a small, small piece of horn so I can carve a new box for my salt?"

"Of course," said the goat kindly, and he lowered his horns until they touched the ground.

The young man took hold of one horn, quickly cut off a small piece, and ran home. As soon as he finished carving his new salt box, he showed it to all his friends in the village. "What a beautiful box!" they cried. "Where did you get it?"

"I carved it myself from a bit of horn that the goat gave me," said the young man.

"What a wonderful idea!" exclaimed the villagers. "Salt is so dear. We must all have boxes of our own to keep it safe."

One little boy standing near the crowd grew worried. "How will the goat make the stars sing if we all take pieces from his horns?"

"No need to worry," said one of the villagers. "The goat has such long, long horns. And we will each take only a small, small piece."

With that, the villagers all rushed off to find the goat. Each one asked the goat for a small, small piece of horn. And the goat, too kind to refuse anyone, meekly lowered his head. One by one, each villager cut off a piece of horn. With each cut, the goat's horns indeed grew shorter and shorter, but the villagers did not notice or care. They could think only about their salt boxes.

The villagers walked home as the sun began to set. They were excited as they began to carve their new boxes. Night fell, and although it was time for bed, no music came from the night sky.

Puzzled, the villagers put down their boxes and looked out their windows. There, on the hill, stood the goat, lifting his head as high as he could into the night sky. But try as he might, he could not tap the stars to make them sing. His golden horns were now too short.

And so the goat stared sadly at the heavens, and all the people of the world went to sleep in silence.

The Small Things We Do Have Meaning

No one will notice. The sad outcome of this tale is the disappearance from the world of a daily magical moment brought about not by some sinister plot, but by a series of small selfish acts, inconsequential alone but with devastating impact when added together. It is about attitude as much as action, and about considering the outcome beyond the immediate benefit to oneself. "Who is wise? One who considers the consequences" (*Talmud, Tamid 32a*).

What makes responsibility a Jewish value? Although Judaism stresses individual freedom of choice in ethical issues, community is central. I must decide for myself what is right and what is wrong. I must also consider what is good or bad for everyone, remembering that I, too, am part of that everyone. "If a person does one good deed . . . the balance of the world is weighted toward the side of merit. And if a person commits a single sin . . . the balance of the world is weighted toward the side of guilt" (*Talmud, Kiddushin 40b*).

The power of community. Turned around, the positive message is one of cooperation: when we work together we can accomplish much more than we can working alone.

The vulnerability of nature. The goat in this story represents the world around us, for the workings of nature can be a source of wonder and delight—especially to young children. The stars do sing, if we listen. But, like the goat who gave to all who asked, nature will not stop us when we mistreat it. There is no built-in device that will ensure our right actions. If I drop litter into a stream, the stream will not stop me. Because the world is at our command, freedom and responsibility are bound up together. It is written in the Midrash that when God put all the world under the care of people, it was with this warning: "Do not corrupt my world; for if you corrupt it, no one will set it right after you" (*Genesis Rabbah 5:10*).

Quizzical Questions

1. What happens when one person picks a flower in a park?

2. What happens when 1,000 people do it?

3. What happens when one person plants a flower in a park?

4. What happens when 1,000 people do it?

Try This!

We can become more aware of our influence in the world when we practice thinking about the consequences of our actions.

Now you try: Play your own version of "What happens?" Make it as silly or serious as you wish.

The Fishing Lesson

any years ago, there lived two fishermen, Simon and Jacob. Although Simon was an old man and Jacob was much younger, they loved to work together, fishing the rivers and lakes near their home. They learned many things from one another.

Early one morning Simon and Jacob stood at the edge of a large lake, and cast their lines into its warm waters. They walked back and forth, casting and pulling, pulling and casting, filling their large baskets with fish to take to the market.

Just as the baskets were nearly full, a man stepped out of the trees near the lake.

"Please, kind gentlemen," the man said to Simon and Jacob. "I am a poor, poor man. I cannot feed myself or my family. Will you help by giving me a fish or two?"

The man was indeed very poor. His clothes were in tatters. He had no shoes. His hair was long and tangled. His fingernails and even his toenails were caked with dirt. And he was so thin that his arms looked like sticks.

Jacob felt sorry for the man. He reached into one of the baskets and began to look for the biggest fish. But before he could pull it out of the basket, Simon stopped him.

"We have no extra fish," said Simon to the man, "but if you go find two long sticks and then come with me, I will teach you how to catch a fish of your own."

The man went back into the trees and found two long, sturdy sticks. Then he came and stood by Simon at the edge of the water.

"Watch me and do what I do," said Simon, taking one of the sticks. With great care, Simon showed the man how to make a fishing pole and a fishing line from the long stick and some string. Simon showed the man how to make a hook from a piece of shell. The man watched Simon closely, and followed every step. When the man became confused, Simon started over and did all the steps again. After several tries, the man finally had a fishing pole of his own.

Then Simon showed the man how to find a worm and put it on his hook. He showed the man how to cast the line far out into the water. The man struggled. The worm fell into the dirt. The hook was slippery. The line got caught on a rock. Each time something went wrong, the man began to mutter in frustration and anger. But patiently, Simon showed the man how to do it, again and again.

It took most of the day, but finally the man felt a tug on his line. A fish! He pulled and pulled on his line until at last, a fat perch flapped onto the shore next to the lake.

"I caught a fish! Look, I caught a fish!" shouted the man gleefully as he jumped up and down with his prize. He pulled a rag out of his tattered coat, wrapped up the fish, and stuffed it down the front of his shirt. He tried to give the fishing pole back to Simon.

"No," said Simon. "You made that pole. It is yours. Tomorrow you can come back and catch another fish."

The man walked off into the wood with his fish and his fishing pole. When he was gone, Jacob turned to Simon. "Why did you make that man work so hard for a fish?"

he said. "We have plenty of fish. We could have given him one of ours and been no poorer ourselves."

"Ah, Jacob," answered Simon. "If we had simply given that man a fish today, he would have been happy and full today. But what will he do when he gets hungry again tomorrow? By teaching him how to catch a fish himself, I showed him how to get food every day for the rest of his life. He and his family need never go hungry again."

We Help by Teaching Others

Teach someone to fish. Judaism often provides a unique synthesis of idealism and practicality, aptly captured by the proverb "Give someone a fish and you feed them for a day. Teach someone to fish, and you feed them for a lifetime." There are two lessons at work here—providing for others in need, and helping them help themselves.

Justice through charity and duty. Tzedakah, the duty to provide for those in need, begins with giving. "Open your hand to your needy kin in your land" (*Deuteronomy 15:11*). In the teachings of Maimonides, tzedakah has eight levels, the highest of which is providing another with the ability to become self-sufficient. Simon's way of helping actually considered the interest of the entire community, not simply the needy man alone. There is no dishonor to being poor, but a person who is self-reliant can also help others. No one is required to impoverish themselves by giving. When more members of the community have the resources to take care of themselves, it helps ensure there will be enough to provide for all.

What makes self-reliance a Jewish value? In addition to outlining our responsibilities to others through tzedakah, Jewish tradition outlines many responsibilities for parents and teachers to guide them in raising children to be strong, independent, and productive. We are told, for example, that a parent must teach a child a trade, and must even teach a child to swim (*Tosefta Kiddushin 1:11*).

Quizzical Questions

1. What did you know how to do when you were a baby?

2. What are three things you can do now?

3. Who taught you?

4. What do you know that you can teach someone else?

Try This!

Everyone knows a song or two (or twenty!). What is your favorite song? How did you learn it?

Now you try: Teach a song you have learned to someone else. Now you can sing together!